This book belongs to

_____

With special thanks to the following people
for their help with translations:

Sylvia Pellarolo, *C.Phil. in Hispanic Languages, U.C.L.A.*
Dominique Abensour, *C.Phil in French and English Languages, U.C.L.A.*
Wolfgang Doering, *C.Phil. in Germanic Languages, U.C.L.A.*

A Rooster Book/September 1994

"Rooster Books" and the portrayal of a rooster are trademarks of
Bantam Doubleday Dell Publishing Group, Inc.

Manufactured in the U.S.A.

Rooster Books are published by Bantam Doubleday Dell Books for Young Readers,
a division of Bantam Doubleday Dell Publishing Group, Inc., 1540 Broadway, New York, NY 10036.

My Clothes

Illustrations by Lisa-Theresa Lenthall

ROOSTER BOOKS

BANTAM DOUBLEDAY DELL
NEW YORK • TORONTO • LONDON • SYDNEY • AUCKLAND

pajamas
(puh-**JAH**-muhz)

el pijama
(ehl pee-**JAH**-mah)

les pyjamas
(lay pih-**JAH**-muh)

der Schlafanzug
(dehr **SHLAHF**-un-tsook)

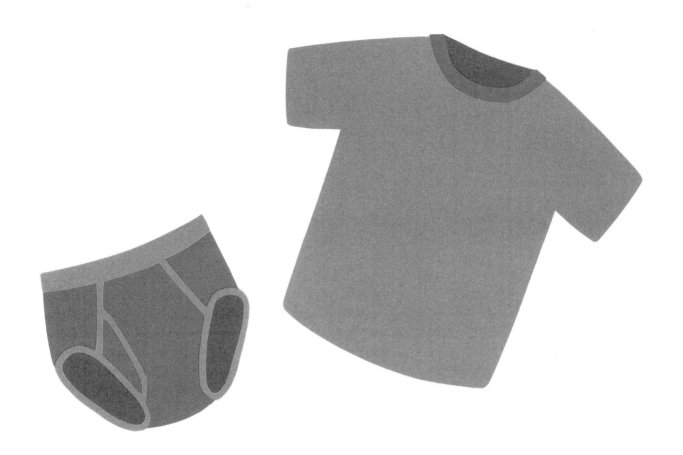

underwear (**UHN**-der-wayr)

la ropa interior (lah **ROH**-pah een-teh-ree-**OR**)

les sous-vêtements (lay soo-**VEHT**-mahn)

die Unterbekleidung (dee **UN**-tuh-buh-kliy-dung)

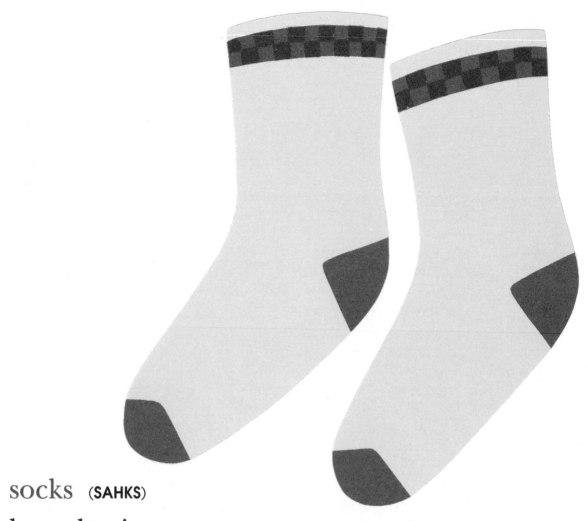

socks (**SAHKS**)

los calcetines (lohs kahl-seh-**TEE**-nehs)

les chaussettes (lay **SHOH**-seht)

die Socken (dee **ZOHK**-kuhn)

shoes (**SHOOZ**)

los zapatos (lohs sah-**PAH**-tohs)

les chaussures (lay **SHOH**-sewr)

die Schuhe (dee **SHOO**-uh)

dress (**DREHS**)

el vestido (ehl vehs-**TEE**-doh)

la robe (lah **ROHB**)

das Kleid (dus **KLIYT**)

skirt (**SKERT**)

la falda (lah **FAHL**-dah)

la jupe (lah **JOOP**)

der Rock (dehr **ROHK**)

blue jeans **(BLOO** jeenz)

los vaqueros (lohs vah-**KEH**-rohs)

blue jeans **(BLOO** jeenz)

die Jeans (dee **JEENS**)

shirt **(SHERT)**

la camisa (lah kah-**MEE**-sah)

la chemise (lah **SHUH**-meez)

das Hemd (dus **HEHMT**)

shorts (**SHORTS**)

los pantalones cortos (lohs pahn-tah-**LOH**-nehs **KOR**-tohs)

les culottes courtes (lay **KOO**-lot koohrt)

die kurze Hose (dee **KOOR**-tsuh **HOH**-zuh)

bathing suit
(**BAYTH**-ihng soot)

el traje de baño
(ehl **TRAH**-heh deh **BAH**-nyoh)

le maillot de bain
(luh **MAH**-yoh duh ban)

der Badeanzug
(dehr **BAH**-duh-un-tsook)

sweater (**SWEHT**-er)

el suéter (ehl **SWEH**-tehr)

le chandail (luh **SHAHN**-diy)

der Pulli (dehr **POOHL**-lih)

scarf **(SKARF)**

la bufanda (lah boo-**FAHN**-dah)

l'écharpe **(LAY**-sharp)

der Schal (dehr **SHAHL**)

boots **(BOOTS)**

las botas (lahs **BOH**-tahs)

les bottes (lay **BUHT**)

die Stiefel (dee **SHTEE**-fuhl)

raincoat (**RAYN**-koht)

el impermeable (ehl eem-pehr-meh-**AH**-bleh)

l'imperméable (lam-pehr-**MAY**-ah-bluh)

der Regenmantel (dehr **RAY**-guhn-mun-tuhl)

hat (**HAT**)

el sombrero (ehl som-**BREH**-roh)

le chapeau (luh shah-**POH**)

der Hut (dehr **HOOT**)

mittens (**MIHT**-uhnz)

los mitones (lohs mee-**TOH**-nehs)

les mitaines (lay **MEE**-tehn)

die Fäustlinge (dee **FOYST**-lihn-guh)

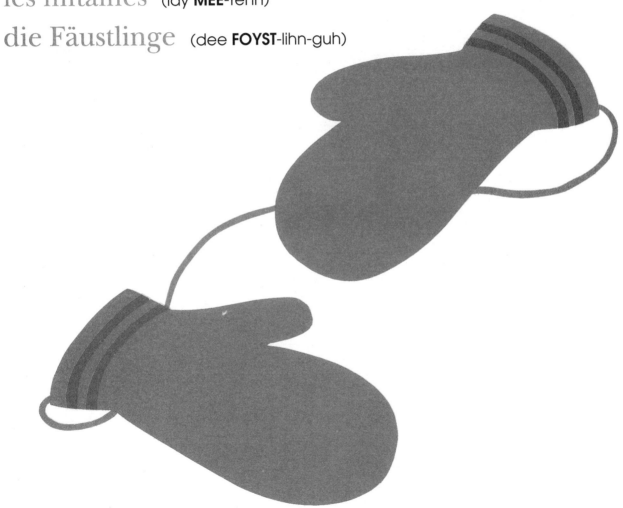